Witness to History

Slavery in the United States

JJ,
10-24-10
ToDAY is your
Mom's BiRthing
DAY Celebrate
PAp pAp

Gary E. Barr

Heinemann Library
Chicago, Illinois

Customer Service 888-454-2279
Visit our website at www.heinemannlibrary.com

Designed by Heinemann Library
Page layout by Ginkgo Creative, Inc.
Photo research by Bill Broyles
Printed and bound in China by South China Printing
Company Limited

08 07 06 05 04
10 9 8 7 6 5 4 3 2 1

**Library of Congress Cataloging-in-Publication
Data**
Barr, Gary, 1951-
    Slavery in the United States / Gary Barr.
        p. cm. -- (Witness to history)
Summary: Uses primary source materials to study the
institution of slavery in the United States and its role in
the Civil War.
Includes bibliographical references (p.) and index.
    ISBN 1-4034-4570-2 (HC) -- ISBN 1-4034-4578-8 (PB)
    1. Slavery--United States--History--Juvenile literature.
2. African Americans--History--Juvenile literature. 3.
Slavery--United States--History--19th century--
Juvenile literature. 4. United States--History--Civil War,
1861-1865--African Americans--Juvenile literature. [1.
Slavery--History--Sources. 2. United States--History--
Civil War, 1861-1865--Sources.] I. Title. II. Witness
to history (Heinemann Library (Firm))
    E441.B343 2004
    973.7′11--dc22
                                        2003018148

Acknowledgments
The author and publisher would like to thank the
following for permission to reproduce photographs:

pp. 4, 37, 48l Library of Congress; pp. 7, 10, 15, 20,
33, 43, 46 Corbis; pp. 8, 12 Mary Evans Picture Library;
pp. 14, 39, 44, 48r National Archives and Records
Administration; pp. 16, 26, 28, 35, 38, 42, 50
Bettmann/Corbis; pp. 18, 22 New York Historical
Society/The Bridgeman Art Library; p. 24 Hulton
Archive/Getty Images; p. 30 William E. Barton
Collection of Lincolniana/Special Collections Research
Center/University of Chicago Library; p. 34 National
Portrait Gallery, Smithsonian Institution/Art Resource,
NY; p. 51 Hulton-Deutsch Collection/Corbis

Cover photograph from 1862 of five generations of
slaves on the Smith's Plantation in Beaufort, South
Carolina, reproduced with permission of Library of
Congress.

The publisher would like to thank Guy LoFaro for his
help in the preparation of this book.

Every effort has been made to contact copyright
holders of any material reproduced in this book. Any
omissions will be rectified in subsequent printings if
notice is given to the publisher.

Disclaimer
All the Internet addresses (URLs) given in this book
were valid at the time of going to press. Due to the
dynamic nature of the Internet, however, some
addresses may have changed, or sites may have ceased
to exist since publication. While the author and
publisher regret any inconvenience this may cause
readers, no responsibility for any such changes can
be accepted by either the author or the publisher.

Some words are shown in bold,
like this. You can find out what
they mean by looking in the glossary.

Contents

Introduction

Only a slave could truly describe the agony of slavery. For 246 years many people in the United States said that slavery was essential to the country's **economy,** and some even praised it. During that same time others tried to end slavery, but could find no concrete solution. Meanwhile, to most African Americans, slavery meant endless work and no freedom.

By the early 1800s, **plantation** owners in the South strongly depended on slave labor. Slaves worked vast fields of cotton, tobacco, sugarcane, and other crops. Planters felt that free labor was the only way to guarantee **profits.** Most masters were not purposely cruel to their slaves—the slaves were too valuable. However, masters frequently ignored how bad their slaves living circumstances really were.

Slavery ended in the North state by state. By 1820, slavery had mostly vanished there. In both the North and the South, numerous whites harshly criticized the practice of slavery, but offered no practical plans

TO BE SOLD, on board the Ship *Bance-Island*, on tuesday the 6th of *May* next, at *Ashley-Ferry*; a choice cargo of about 250 fine healthy

NEGROES,

just arrived from the Windward & Rice Coast. —The utmost care has already been taken, and shall be continued, to keep them free from the least danger of being infected with the SMALL-POX, no boat having been on board, and all other communication with people from *Charles-Town* prevented.

Austin, Laurens, & Appleby.

N. B. Full one Half of the above Negroes have had the SMALL-POX in their own Country.

This is a newspaper ad describing slaves shipped from Africa that will be sold in Charleston (Charles-Town), South Carolina.

for ending it. The main course of action proposed was an immediate end to slavery. But with many plantation owners paying huge sums of money to acquire and care for slaves, how could they suddenly give up this source of wealth and labor?

While **abolitionists** and supporters of slavery argued with each other, slaves toiled in the fields. From "can see to can't see"—sunrise to sundown—work was the rule, six days a week. "Being a slave was no better than being a dog," one former slave wrote. Another slave stated, "I was constantly grieving and pining, and wishing for death, rather than anything else."

Despite the system of **bondage** that enslaved them, African-American slaves survived and even created their own culture. They raised families, educated their children, and passed on **traditions.** It was difficult under their current conditions, but they found a way to make life as rewarding as they possibly could.

How would you have resisted if you were a slave? Several methods of resistance were tried to combat slavery. Some resistance methods were carried out on a very small scale, while others involved huge **rebellions.** None of the large-scale attempts to **revolt** succeeded in the United States, but countless lesser forms of resistance worked well.

Why was this cruelty allowed to continue? What attempts were made to end slavery in the United States? What was it like to be a slave? Explore the answers to these questions and more from the viewpoint of those who lived during the time of slavery. Learn how rebellions, **protests,** and government actions all failed and resulted in the American Civil War (1861–1865). Hear the words of slaves as they struggled to survive.

How Do We Know?

By studying history, we can learn about past events. For example, if we need to find out about the fall of the **Roman Empire** or the Norman invasion of England, we can find many books and articles about these subjects. Books and articles can tell us when and how the events took place and provide details about the important people. Books and articles often not only explain why things have happened by examining the background of the events, but also how the events shaped the course of history.

Although books and articles can be helpful and informative, they are often written many years—sometimes hundreds of years—after the events they describe. And, like any story that is told secondhand, some changes, and even mistakes, can creep into the accounts. Perhaps a historian did not like Romans or military leaders. Such an attitude can affect how a historian tells a story. A historian may present the facts as he or she wanted them to occur. A historian might leave out facts that do not fit into his or her worldview. Such a personal opinion is called **bias,** and it makes some historical accounts unreliable.

On the other hand, a historian might have no personal opinion on the matter. However, he or she still relies on accounts that were written long after the events. Such accounts are called secondary sources because a historian arrives at them secondhand. Historians who base their writing on earlier retellings might repeat the bias or even the mistakes of the previous accounts. It is easy to see how this process can change a simple statement with each retelling.

Getting to the source

Primary sources are firsthand accounts of events. Historians researching events from long ago must rely on primary sources such as codes of law, parish registers, letters, journals, and diaries. Using these resources to tell the story of slavery in the United States is a challenge. Most people had strong opinions about slavery, so descriptions without bias are rare. The time of slavery ended before modern communication tools were used. Usually firsthand accounts, particularly those of slaves, were written after the time period. In recent times, extensive research has attempted to improve our knowledge of what actually happened.

The purpose of history

Studying history helps us learn how humans coped with various problems. By studying history we learn how to face similar problems in today's world and possible issues in the future. At first, history books told the story of slavery from the perspective of white people. As time progressed, however, slaves were able to tell their own stories through interviews, diaries, and other sources.

Many former slaves gave interviews or wrote their experiences down. These written records are priceless sources for historians.

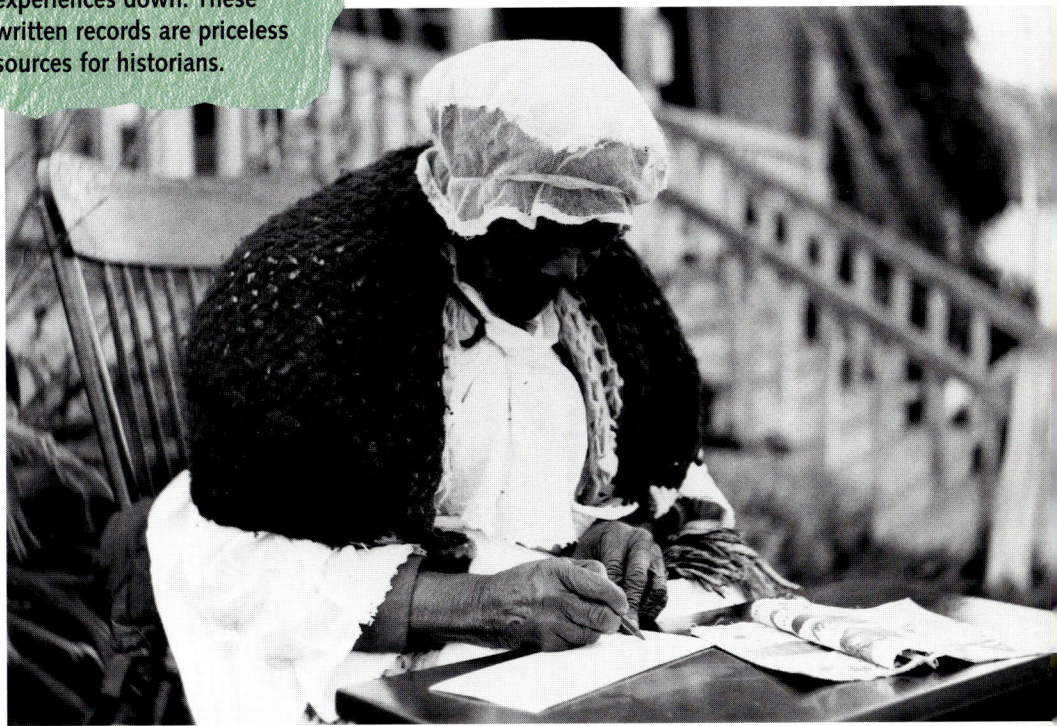

What Is Slavery?

A slave is a person who is owned by another person. Slaves are forced to work for their owners without pay. In the United States, most slaves usually remained slaves for their entire lives. Slave owners often provided food, clothing, and shelter. However, they had almost no other responsibility for a slave's welfare.

Slavery in history

Slavery has existed for thousands of years. It has existed in most inhabited lands at some time or another, including ancient Egypt, ancient China, and among Indians in Mexico. People who had the most power often placed **prisoners of war** in **bondage.** Sometimes they would enslave people of a different **race** or people who were poor. The relationship was typically that of a master and an animal or a piece of property.

Indentured servants

The British colonies in North America were constantly short of labor. Some people who had trouble finding work in Great Britain would agree to become **indentured servants.** A wealthy person would pay for an indentured servant's passage on a ship, provide for his or her basic needs, and expect him or her to work for four to seven years. After the time period of work was done, indentured servants were free. They could then start a new life that probably would not have been possible in Great Britain. The great majority of indentured servants coming to the British colonies in North America were white Europeans. When the very first Africans arrived in Jamestown, Virginia, in 1619, they were considered to be indentured servants, not slaves.

Slavery is not a new practice. Different cultures around the world have practiced slavery. Here, a 17th-century Turkish slave is being branded.

William Buckland's indenture contract

In 1755, 22-year-old William Buckland agreed to become an indentured servant for Thomas Mason for a period of four years. The contract was signed in London, England, but stated that both men would travel to Mason's **plantation** in Virginia.

This Indenture . . . Between William Buckland . . . and Thomas Mason of London . . . That He the said William Buckland shall and will, as a faithful **Covenant** Servant, well and truly serve the said Thomas Mason . . . in the Plantation of Virginia beyond the Seas, for the Space of Four Years. . . . And the said Thomas Mason . . . shall and will at the like Costs and Charges, provide for and allow the said Wm [William] Buckland all necessary . . . Meat, Drink, Washing, Lodging . . . as Covenant Servants in such Cases are usually provided for . . .

Richard Allen's account

Richard Allen was a slave who lived in Delaware during the 1700s. He wrote a brief, informative description of his life. Later, he was able to buy his freedom and return to Philadelphia, Pennsylvania. Mr. Allen was deeply religious and eventually became a preacher.

I was born in the year of our Lord 1760, on February 14th, a slave to Benjamin Chew, of Philadelphia. My mother and father and four children of us were sold into Delaware state, near Dover . . . I had it often impressed upon my mind [told to me] that I should one day enjoy my freedom; for slavery is a bitter pill [hard to take], notwithstanding we had a good master. But when we would think that our day's work was never done, we often thought that after our master's death we were liable [likely] to be sold to the highest bidder, as he was much in **debt** . . . I was often brought to weep between the porch and the altar.

Slavery Begins in English America

A constant problem in early America was a shortage of labor. In 1619, the first Africans were brought to Virginia. They were sold or traded by Dutch seamen to colonists in Jamestown, and were considered to be **indentured servants.** Little is known about these Africans and their lives. But their arrival was a significant event because slavery in the United States eventually became almost entirely based on African labor.

Why Africans?

European settlers tried to enslave Native Americans. However, Native Americans did not make good slaves—they died of European diseases or lacked the necessary farming skills. Many of the Africans brought to the British colonies by slave traders had experience farming crops in their homelands. The invention of the **cotton gin** in 1793 only increased the need for laborers to grow and pick cotton.

In the 1600s and 1700s, slave traders found ways to make large **profits.** Factory goods from Great Britain and other European nations would be traded for slaves. Slaves were then traded for goods from the New World. These goods were then sold in Great Britain. Since the trading ship routes often traced a triangle shape on maps, this system became known as Triangular Trade.

To ensure that the slave labor force remained intact and even increased in size, **plantation** owners lobbied for stricter laws. These laws not only made it more difficult to free slaves, but also said that the children of slaves born in the colonies automatically became enslaved themselves. As the colonies expanded westward, the need for more and more slaves increased.

This painting depicts a Dutch slave ship arriving at Jamestown, Virginia, in 1619.

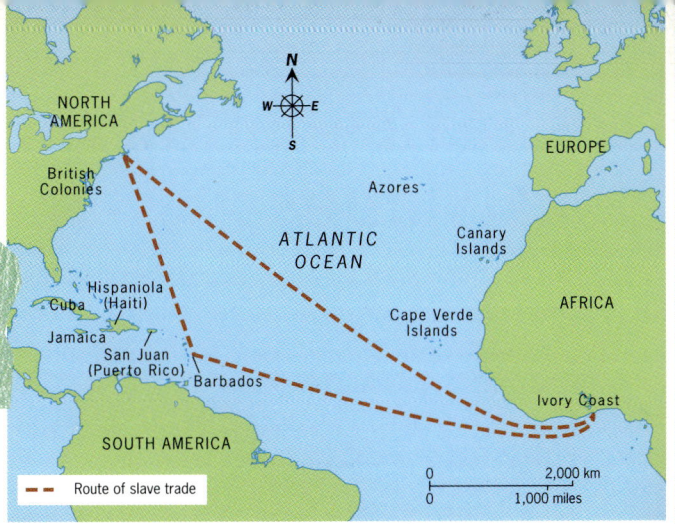

This map shows the Triangular Trade route that trading ships took when transporting slaves and other goods.

John Rolfe's letter

John Rolfe, a Virginian, is most famous for marrying Pocahontas and making tobacco farms **profitable**. Below is part of a letter Rolfe wrote in January 1619 to a fellow colonist named Edwin Sandys regarding the first Africans to land at Jamestown, Virginia.

August. The first African slaves are brought to Virginia by Captain Jope in a Dutch ship. Governor Yeardley and a merchant, Abraham Piersey, exchange twenty of them for supplies. These Africans become indentured servants like the white indentured servants who traded passage [to North America] for **servitude.**

A new law in Virginia

The status of blacks in Virginia slowly changed over the last half of the 17th century. In 1705, a law passed by the Virginia General Assembly removed any doubts about who was considered a slave.

All servants imported and brought into the Country . . . who were not Christians in their native Country . . . shall be accounted and be slaves. All Negro, **mulatto** and Indian slaves within this dominion [area] . . . shall be held to be real estate [property]. If any slave resist his master . . . correcting [punishing] such slave, and shall happen to be killed in such correction . . . the master shall be free of all punishment . . . as if such accident never happened.

Capture and Transport of Slaves

Most of the Africans transported to the British colonies in North America came from West and Central Africa. The name given to the sea voyage from Africa to the Caribbean Islands was the Middle Passage. It was called the Middle Passage because it was the second, or middle, of three parts of the Triangular Trade. To maximize **profits,** slaves were tightly packed into several decks of a ship. The hot, crowded, unhealthy conditions caused illness and disease. Countless slaves did not survive the 4,000-mile [6,437-kilometer] trip across the Atlantic Ocean.

Before arriving in the colonies, slaves were taken to the **West Indies.** There, they were taught how to speak some English. Slaves were also given farm training if they did not already have it. Some slaves were put to work on large **plantations** built on the West Indies. The rest journeyed to North America.

The final stage of the journey was from the West Indies to one of the major **ports** of the colonies. Here slaves would be held until they were sold to the highest bidder during an **auction.** Some of the main ports accepting slaves were New Orleans, Louisiana; Boston, Massachusetts; Charleston, South Carolina; and Alexandria, Virginia. In 1808, it became illegal to bring slaves into the United States from Africa. But by that time, millions of slaves had already arrived.

Many people were captured in wars between African kingdoms and sold to slave traders. Others were kidnapped and forced onto slave ships.

An African prince's account

James Albert Ukawsaw Gronniosaw was an African prince. Below, he remembers his homeland and describes how a merchant kidnapped him.

I was born in the city of Barnou [in present-day Nigeria], my mother was the eldest daughter of the reigning King . . . There came a merchant from the Gold Coast . . . he expressed vast concern for me, and said, if my parents would part with me for a little while, and let him take me home with him, it would be of more service to me than anything they could do for me . . . I was now more than a thousand miles [1,600 kilometers] from home . . . A few days after a Dutch ship came into the harbour, and they carried me on board, in hopes that the Captain would purchase me. As they went, I heard them agree, that, if they could not sell me then, they would throw me overboard.

A captain's account

Reverend John Newton was a slaving captain before he became a minister. He described the accommodations for slaves on a slave-trading ship.

Their lodging rooms below the deck which are three besides a place for the sick, are sometimes more than five feet [1.5 meters] high and sometimes less; and this height is divided toward the middle for the slaves to lie in two rows, one above the other, on each side of the ship, close to each other like books upon a shelf . . . The poor creatures, thus cramped, are likewise in irons for the most part which makes it difficult for them to turn or move or attempt to rise or to lie down without hurting themselves or each other. Every morning, perhaps, more instances than one are found of the living and the dead fastened together.

A Slave Auction

After slaves landed at United States **ports,** a ship captain would be paid for bringing them from Africa and the **West Indies. Slave traders** who specialized in buying and selling slaves then took over. Slaves were made to appear as attractive as possible for their coming sale.

In port cities, there was usually a specific place called a **slave block.** This is where slaves were displayed and put on sale. Usually a slave block was a small, raised stage on which potential buyers could clearly see the people being sold. One at a time, slaves were put on the stage while an **auctioneer** described their qualities. Then, bids were taken.

Before potential buyers bought a slave, they would usually step onto the slave block. Often buyers would examine a slave's health by looking at his or her teeth and making him or her partially undress. A buyer would even tell a slave to jump or dance to show he or she could move well. Sometimes the crowd would cruelly taunt slaves while this was being done.

Often times, slave **auctions** were so emotionally agonizing that **plantation** owners avoided auctions by paying an **agent** to buy slaves for them. The owners knew that slaves feared being sold away from their families. They often threatened slaves with this possibility in order to ensure obedience. Most slaves said they preferred **floggings** to being sold away from their families.

While waiting to be sold at auction, slaves were kept in cells like this one. Poor sanitary conditions in such places and on slave ships caused large amounts of African slaves to die of disease.

The threat of being sold
William Wells Brown, a slave employed by slave traders, wrote a description of a slave auction.

There was in this lot a number of old men and women, some them with gray locks [hair] . . . I was ordered to have the old men's whiskers shaved off, and the gray hairs plucked out where they were not too numerous, in which case he had a preparation of blacking [dye] to color it . . . This was new business to me, and was performed in a room where the passengers could not see us . . . and after going through the blacking process, they looked ten or fifteen years younger.

In a short time the **planters** came flocking to the pen to purchase slaves . . . Some [slaves] were set to dancing, some to jumping, some to singing, and some to playing cards. This was done to make them appear cheerful and happy. My business was to see that they were placed in those situations before the arrival of the purchasers, and I have often set them to dancing when their cheeks were wet with tears.

Some slave parents could only watch as their children were sold to a different buyer. When this happened, parents usually never saw their sons and daughters again.

Masters and Overseers

A slave owner was known as a master. On large **plantations,** masters needed help and would hire an **overseer.** Overseers were managers who made sure that slaves did their work properly.

An overseer would either be a white man employed by the slave owner or a slave who received extra **rations** and benefits for supervising the other slaves. Overseers had a very difficult job. On one hand, overseers had to motivate people being held against their will to work. On the other hand, they had to protect the expensive property (slaves) of their master.

Owners of smaller plantations often worked side-by-side with their slaves. Slaves would sometimes gain more respect and better treatment from this close relationship. However, small farmers sometimes could not provide for their slaves as well.

Most plantation owners tried to take care of a slave's basic needs and motivated their labor force through a system of rewards. This was because they realized that slaves were too expensive and valuable to be treated otherwise. However, some owners felt that the high prices they paid for their slaves gave them the right to treat them any way they wished. Some abused their slaves in the most unspeakable ways.

Overseers varied widely in their treatment of slaves. Some overseers were brutal, but some were respected by masters and tolerated by slaves.

Edmund Bacon's memories
Edmund Bacon was the slave overseer for Thomas Jefferson, who was the third president of the United States.

Mr. Jefferson was always very kind and indulgent [generous] to his servants [slaves]. He would not allow them to be at all overworked, and he would hardly ever allow one of them to be whipped. His orders to me were constant, that if there was any servant that could not be got along with without the chastising [scolding] that was customary, to dispose of him. He could not bear to have a servant whipped, no odds [matter] how much he deserved it.

A slave's opinion
Mingo White was a slave on a plantation in Alabama. Below, he describes the attitudes of his master and overseer.

It was hard back in them days. Every morning before daybreak you had to be up and ready to get to the field. After a day's work, there wasn't anything for the slaves to do but go to bed . . . Every night the drivers [overseers] come around to make sure that we was in the bed . . . The white folks didn't teach us to do anything but work. They said we weren't supposed to know how to read and write.

> " He must be *made* to work, and should always be given to understand that if he fails to perform his duty he will be punished for it. "
> Arkansas slave owner.

Work

On large **plantations** there were three classes of slaves: field hands, craftsmen, and house servants. Each of these classes performed different tasks and received different levels of respect.

The field hands worked from "can see to can't see," or from sunrise until sundown. Their work was far from the main house and supervised by **overseers.** Field hands cleared land, worked the soil, and picked crops. They regularly worked outside in extremely hot— and sometimes cold—conditions. Their work was the hardest of all slave work and they were most at risk for brutal treatment.

Craftsmen, such as blacksmiths, carpenters, and cooks, had skills vital to the smooth functioning of a plantation. These slaves made up the **industrial** community of a plantation. As plantation owners had free labor, they attempted to be **self-sufficient** by having slaves manufacture all the goods a plantation needed. In some cases, the goods made by slaves would be sold for **profit.** Because of their trained skills, craftsmen were respected more than field hands.

Slaves who received the most respect and had the best working conditions were house servants. House servants usually had nicer clothes than the other slaves, and their work in the main house was not as physical. However, house servants had to be available 24 hours a day. For example, if someone in the master's family became ill during the night, the house servants had to go and help.

This slave family stops picking cotton to pose for a picture. They worked on a plantation near Savannah, Georgia, in the 1860s.

Olaudah Equiano's account

Olaudah Equiano was born in 1745, far from the African coast in a remote part of the Kingdom of Benin. His father was a respected government official in his **province**. Equiano was captured and made a slave at the age of eight, but he eventually gained his freedom. He left behind a detailed description of his life.

We were landed up a river a good way from the sea, about Virginia country, where we saw few of our native Africans, and not one soul who could talk to me. I was a few weeks weeding grass and gathering stones in a plantation; and at last all my companions were distributed different ways, and only myself was left. I was now exceedingly [very] miserable . . . but I had no person to speak to that I could understand. In this state I was constantly grieving and pining, and wishing for death rather than anything else.

Austin Steward remembers

Austin Steward was a slave from 1820 to 1842. He was later freed and lived to be 62 years old.

When I was eight years of age, I was taken to the "great house," or the family mansion of my master, to serve as an errand boy, where I had to stand in the presence of my master's family all the day, and a part of the night, ready to do any thing which they commanded me to perform.

When I was not employed as an errand boy, it was my duty to stand behind my master's chair, which was sometimes the whole day, never being allowed to sit in his presence . . . If a slave is addressed when sitting, he is required to spring to his feet, and instantly remove his hat, if he has one, and answer in the most humble manner, or lay the foundation [give cause] for a flogging, which will not be long delayed.

Women and Children

Male and female slaves often had separate jobs. Both men and women worked in the fields, helped with gardens, and acted as house servants. But most other tasks were separate.

Women sewed, cooked, cared for the master's children, and did the housework. Slave mothers had little time to pay attention to their own families. Some slaves said that when they were children, they almost never saw their mothers. Children would be asleep when their mother left for work and when she came home. Some women had to get up at 3:00 A.M. and did not get home until well after dark. Older slave women often provided childcare for both white and black children. These women were called mammys. White children sometimes became so attached to their mammys that they formed close relationships that lasted for the rest of their lives.

Slave children had few tasks until they were about ten years old, although all children helped during harvesttime. Until that age, many slave children did not realize they were any different from the white children of the household. They played and took part in activities much like white children. Eventually, a master's family would begin to train their children by telling them to give orders to the slave children. This often came as a surprise to the slave children, but made them soon realize that they were not the same as their white friends.

Mammys acted as mothers in that they would raise their masters' children like their own.

Harriet Newby's letter

Harriet Newby's husband was freed. In the following letter, she pleads with him to return and buy her freedom.

Dear husband,

I want you to buy me as soon as possible, for if you do not get me somebody else will … Dear husband, you [know] not the trouble I see. … It is said Master is in want of money. If so, I know not what time he may sell me, and then all my bright hopes of the future are blasted, for there has been one bright hope to cheer me in all my troubles, that is to be with you … Do all you can for me, which I have no doubt you will.

Your affectionate wife,

Harriet Newby

Childhood memories

Mary Island of Louisiana remembers her childhood on a **plantation**.

Washing dishes when I was four years old. When I was six I carried water. When I got to be seven years old, I was cutting sprouts almost like a man, and when I was eight, I could pick one hundred pounds [45 kilograms] of cotton.

Food, Clothing, and Shelter

Masters were supposed to provide for the basic needs of their slaves: food, clothing, and shelter. It was in a master's best interest to keep his or her slaves healthy so they could work. However, many masters tried to save money by providing slaves with low-quality food, clothing, and shelter.

Often times, slaves did not complain much about the quantities of food **rations** they received, though they were opposed to the lack of variety in their food. Slave mothers had to be creative when preparing meals with the unchanging supplies of corn, pork, and flour they received. Sometimes slaves were permitted to plant gardens and hunt and fish in their free time, and this helped supplement their diet. Slaves would even trade goods to masters for extra supplies.

Slaves usually received two sets of clothing: one set to wear in warm weather, and one set to wear in cold weather. Slaves had to repair or clean their clothes themselves. Sometimes they wore the same clothing until it fell apart.

Most slave cabins were simple, crowded, and poorly constructed. The cabins were made of wood, but many did not keep out the cold or rain very well. An entire cabin was usually made up of one room with a dirt floor and no windows. As many as eight people might live in a space the size of a small bedroom in today's houses.

One slave remembered that the cabin "did not keep the cold out, but kept the smoke from the fireplace in."

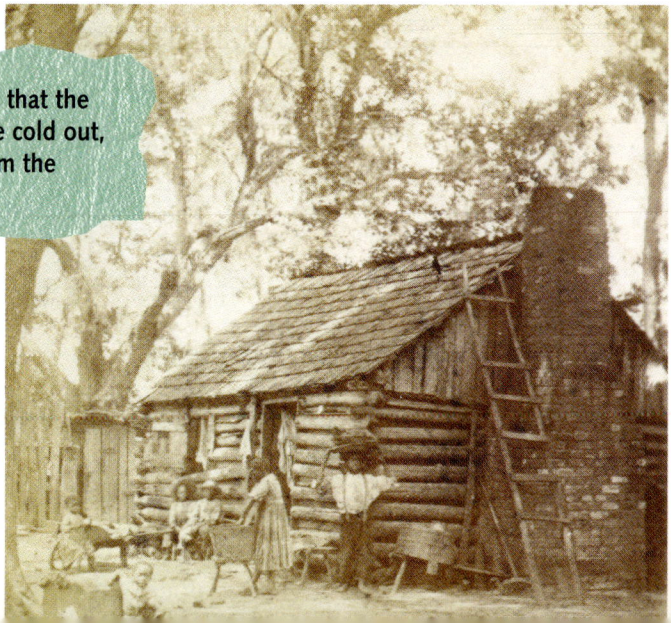

Mary Reynolds's interview

Mary Reynolds lived on a Louisiana **plantation** as a slave in the mid-1800s. While still a slave, she was married. Mary and her groom stood outside a cabin door in front of witnesses. They stepped across a broomstick, went into the cabin, and they were married. After the Civil War, Mrs. Reynolds was freed. She told her story to an interviewer when she was 99 years old. In the following excerpt, the interviewer recalls what Ms. Reynolds said about her cabin.

Mary lived in the slave cabins with her parents and brothers and sisters. Her cabin was better than the average. "It was nice and warm," she remembered. It was made of pine boards and had a fireplace. Many slave quarters did not have a fireplace. The beds in Mary's cabin were boards attached to the wall, covered with a mattress stuffed with shucks, the stiff leaves taken off ears of corn. At night the men would sometimes find the time and material to make chairs for the cabins. That was all the furniture Mary remembered. . . . They had a garden patch behind the cabins. . . . Clothes were washed in the creek on Saturday night and hung in the woods to dry.

James Bolton's experience

James Bolton was a slave on a plantation in Oglethorpe County, Georgia. He described his living conditions.

We stayed in a one-room cabin with a dirt floor. A frame made out of pine poles was fastened to the wall to hold up the mattresses. Our mattresses was made out of cotton bagging stuffed with wheat straw. Our covers was quilts made out of old clothes. Slave women too old to work in the fields made the quilts . . . They [masters] allowanced us a week's ration at a time. It were generally hog meat [pork], corn meal, and sometimes a little flour.

Slave Families

A slave's family life was very difficult because of the long work hours and restricted freedom. Often, it was hard for a slave to find a husband or wife. Slaves usually married someone they met on their own **plantation.** Sometimes slaves visited or worked on other, nearby farms and would meet their future spouses there. Typically, marriage ceremonies were simple and involved the couple pledging their love to each other in front of witnesses. By the 1800s, Southern states made slave marriages illegal, but slaves continued to marry following their own customs.

Families were extremely important to slaves. When a slave got his or her freedom, he or she would often work—sometimes for several years—so he or she could pay for his or her spouse to be freed too.

How do you think your family could cope if you were slaves? You would be confronted by poor housing, long hours of work, punishment, and separation from close relatives. Many slaves who **rebelled** did so as a reaction to such situations. Conditions were bad enough that several slave husbands said they married women from separate plantations on purpose. They could not bear watching their wives and children being punished or abused in other ways by plantation owners or **overseers.** In situations like this, a family only gathered on Saturday nights and Sundays, when slaves usually had time off.

Parents taught children life skills, passed on stories of their ancestors, and in many cases, encouraged them to gain their freedom.

Harriet Jacobs's experience

Harriet Jacobs was born a slave in Edenton, North Carolina. Her book, *Incidents in the Life of a Slave Girl, Written by Herself,* convinced many people to support the **liberation** of slaves during the Civil War.

When I was six years old, my mother died; and then, for the first time, I learned, by the talk around me, that I was a slave. . . . I now entered on my fifteenth year—a sad epoch [time] in the life of a slave girl. My master began to whisper foul words in my ear . . . I turned from him with disgust and hatred. But he was my master . . . He told me I was his property; that I must be subject to his will in all things . . . The degradation [moral decline], the wrongs, the vices, that grow out of slavery, are more than I can describe.

Separation

Hannah Chapman was separated from her father. He was sold to a neighboring plantation.

That was a sad time for us … [My father] missed us and we longed for him. He would often sneak back for visits. We would gather round him and crawl up in his lap happy as we could be.

The Community

On large **plantations** slaves came together to support one another. Slave cabins were often very close to each other, and the cabins formed a little village. Slaves had limited time for socialization, since they spent most of their waking hours working, and because masters were fearful that their slaves, if gathered, would plot against them. Despite this, the slave community performed important functions.

Free speech with whites was not permitted in most cases. For example, slaves usually were not allowed to look directly at a white person, and were required to bow their heads and speak in a humble tone. If they did otherwise, they risked punishment. But within the slave community, they could talk freely. This was a relief and comfort. Escape plans and other ways to resist were often planned during evening gatherings.

Older slaves were respected and frequently sought out by other slaves for advice. Some plantation owners made such slave leaders **overseers** if they could. The slave overseer and his family were usually given extra **rations** and a nicer house. Popular slave leaders were sometimes able to create working conditions that were more tolerable for the other slaves than could have been provided by a white overseer.

Most slaves converted to Christianity, but many also continued to practice the religions they had followed in their African homelands. In these religions there was often a powerful figure known as the conjurer. It was believed that the conjurer could cast spells, heal, and perform other supernatural actions.

A group of slaves gathered outside a cabin for this picture. Slaves used these gatherings for socializing and for plotting escapes.

Escape!

William Craft and his wife Ellen thought of a way to escape from their plantation. The following description tells about the beginning of their escape.

Knowing that slaveholders have the privledge of taking their slaves to any part of the country they think proper, it occurred to me that, as my wife was nearly white, I might get her to disguise herself as an invalid gentleman, and assume to be my master, while I could attend as his slave, and that in this manner we might effect our escape.

Just before the time arrived, in the morning, for us to leave, I cut off my wife's hair square at the back of the head, and got her to dress in the disguise and stand out on the floor. I found that she made a most respectable looking gentleman.

We opened the door, and stepped as softly out as "moonlight upon the water." I locked the door with my own key, which I now have before me, and tiptoed across the yard into the street. I say tiptoed, because we were like persons near a tottering avalanche, afraid to move, or even breathe freely, for fear the sleeping tyrants [master and overseer] should be aroused, and come down upon us with double vengence, for daring to attempt to escape in the manner which we contemplated [thought].

Gus Smith's experience

Gus Smith was a slave in Missouri. The work was very hard, but he was lucky because his master allowed many activities on the plantation.

My master let us come and go pretty much as we pleased. In fact, we had much more freedom than most of the slaves had in those days. He let us go to other places to work when we had nothing to do at home, and we kept our money we earned and spent it to suit ourselves . . . We had quiltings, dancing, and making rails for days at a time . . . White folks and colored folks came to these gatherings from miles around, stay up all night dancing, eating, and drinking.

Time Off from Work

Almost all masters gave slaves a break from Saturday evening until Monday morning. Slaves used their free time to complete household chores, socialize, and enjoy entertainment.

Sometimes slaves were allowed to have gardens. They would supplement their diets with the vegetables they grew. In some cases, they could even sell extra food to masters. Male slaves also tried to help by hunting or catching fish. Female slaves did housework, made clothes, and performed numerous other tasks during this time.

Storytelling, music, races, wrestling, and other activities were popular forms of entertainment. Storytelling was influenced by **traditions** handed down from one generation to the next, and often included African themes.

Music also contained African themes. Songs commonly expressed the hopes and beliefs of slaves. African-American spirituals—a form of music that combined religious beliefs with hopes for the future—grew out of this music. The music that slaves created had a secondary purpose. It often had a strong rhythm that accompanied slave work.

When slaves did not have access to musical instruments, they created their own. Some of America's greatest folk music came from such creativity.

"Swing Low, Sweet Chariot"

"Swing Low, Sweet Chariot," a song with its roots in slavery before the American Civil War, is still a popular song today.

Swing low, sweet chariot
Comin' for to carry me home
Swing low, sweet chariot
Comin' for to carry me home

I looked over Jordan and what did I see
Comin' for to carry me home
A band of angels comin' after me
Comin' for to carry me home

Swing low, sweet chariot
Comin' for to carry me home
Swing low, sweet chariot
Comin' for to carry me home

If you get to heaven before I do
Comin' for to carry me home
Tell all my friends I'm comin' there too
Comin' for to carry me home

Swing low, sweet chariot
Comin' for to carry me home
Swing low, sweet chariot
Comin' for to carry me home

I'm sometimes up and sometimes down
Comin' for to carry me home
But still I know I'm heavenly (freedom) bound
Comin' for to carry me home

Swing low, sweet chariot
Comin' for to carry me home
Swing low, sweet chariot
Comin' for to carry me home

If I get there before you do
Comin' for to carry me home
I'll cut a hole and pull you through
Comin' for to carry me home

Swing low, sweet chariot
Comin' for to carry me home
Swing low, sweet chariot
Comin' for to carry me home

29

Government Debate and Policy

From the 1600s—when America consisted of British colonies—to the 1850s, government officials in both the North and the South struggled with the issue of slavery. During this time, most laws and government actions concerned with slavery occurred at the colony or state level. In the late 1700s, Northern states began to **abolish** slavery. They called upon Southern states to do the same. Between 1796–1804, slaves in what is now Haiti carried out a successful **revolt** against their owners. This event caused an intense fear of slave **rebellions** in the United States. State **legislatures** in the South responded by making slave laws, which governed the lives of slaves, much stricter.

When the United States wrote the Constitution in 1787, it permitted slavery to continue in the South. As the years passed, support for abolition among Northern states continued to grow. Representatives from the North proposed solution after solution to the problem of slavery. None worked.

As settlers pushed farther west toward California, several compromises were created to keep either side from dominating the vote on slavery and related issues. Henry Clay was the author of several of the most important agreements. By the 1850s, representatives from the North and the South became more and more radical in their views over the issue. The U.S. began to fall apart and divide into two segments. This would eventually lead to **secession** by the South and plunge the nation into Civil War.

Henry Clay became known as the Great Compromisor. Most of his agreements worked for a short time before both sides began to argue again.

Abraham Lincoln speaks

Abraham Lincoln was an **abolitionist** long before he became president of the United States in 1861. Below, he shares some of his thoughts on slavery.

No man is good enough to govern another man without that other's consent.

-October 16, 1854

"A house divided against itself cannot stand." I believe this government cannot endure permanently half slave and half free. I do not expect the union to be dissolved—I do not expect the house to fall—but I do expect it will cease to be divided. It will become all one thing, or all the other.

-June 16, 1858

As I would not be a *slave*, so I would not be a *master*. This expresses my idea of democracy. Whatever differs from this, to the extent of the difference, is no democracy.

-August 1, 1858

This is a world of compensations; and he who would be no slave must consent to have no slave. Those who deny freedom to others deserve it not for themselves, and, under a just God, cannot long retain it.

-April 6, 1859

Southern Attitudes and the Defense of Slavery

The wealthy southerners who controlled politics in the South had become dependent on slavery and defended it in various ways. But attitudes of other southerners toward slavery varied. Most southerners accepted slavery as a necessary evil that allowed **agriculture** to be **profitable.** They tried to ignore how bad the practice of slavery was.

Many supporters of slavery stated that circumstances for slaves in the South were not as bad as circumstances for poor factory workers in the North. It was true that Northern laborers faced poor living conditions and very low wages. Supporters of slavery pointed out that Southern **plantations** were producing valuable, essential goods such as cotton, tobacco, and food. They said that slaves were needed because it would be too expensive to pay the countless people needed to work plantations.

A common belief among Southern whites was that Africans lacked important abilities as humans. This racial **prejudice** led Southern whites to feel they could treat Africans as property. Most slave owners were better to their slaves than Northerners perceived, but the condition of slavery itself was mentally abusive. Many people think that this mental **manipulation** was one of the worst things that plantation owners did. Southern slave owners used rewards and punishments to motivate, control, and maintain loyalty among their slaves.

Paternalism was used to make slaves dependent upon the plantation owner. Owners constantly stressed to slaves the benefits they received working on the plantation, such as housing, food, and clothing. They warned slaves of the dangers in the world outside the plantation. Additionally, most slave owners deprived slaves of education to make them more helpless. These tactics made a lot of slaves believe they could not survive without their owner's help. Meanwhile, it was common for plantation owners to boast of how happy their slaves were, overlooking the many problems slaves faced.

Excerpts from a slave code
The Alabama Slave Code of 1852 outlined a series of laws that applied to slaves only.

1. Every slave who breaks into and enters a dwelling house in the night time, with the intention to steal or commit a felony, must, on conviction, suffer death.

2. No slave must go beyond the limits of the plantation on which he [or she] resides, without a pass, or some letter from his [or her] master or overseer.

3. No slave can keep or carry a gun, powder, shot, club, or other weapon . . .

4. No slave can own property.

James Madison's idea
James Madison wrote to a friend of how racial prejudice had overcome whites in the United States.

If I could work a miracle, I know what it would be. I would make all the blacks white; and then I could do away with slavery in twenty-four hours.

This political cartoon from 1859 depicts the conflict between Governor Henry Wise of Virginia (a Southern state) and a group of **abolitionists.**

Northern Attitudes

Northern states **abolished** slavery early. The **Quakers** were some of the first **abolitionists** in America. The Quaker religion states that all people should be treated equally. Some Quakers made formal requests to the United States government asking that slaves be freed. Others worked secretly to help slaves escape to freedom.

In the North, women's groups also began to **protest** and press for the **liberation** of slaves in the South. Great speakers and writers such as Harriet Beecher Stowe, Frederick Douglass, Louisa May Alcott, Walt Whitman, and William Lloyd Garrison pleaded for action to be taken. As the years wore on, abolitionists believed that they were fighting against what they called the "moral wrong of slavery."

Frederick Douglass was a freed slave. His mother was a slave and his father was a **plantation** owner. After his master freed him, he pursued an education. Part of his schooling was in Europe, where he lived for two years. He returned to the United States and was a convincing writer and speaker in the fight against slavery.

The **Republican Party** was founded in the 1850s as an antislavery political group. The Party's support quickly grew in popularity, as it was well-organized in both the north and the west. Though defeated by Democrats in the presidential election of 1856, the Republicans gained the office four years later when Abraham Lincoln won. The Republican Party dominated the presidency and Congress for the next twenty years, and held almost all power in the North during the Civil War.

People who previously thought blacks were inferior changed their minds when they saw how talented and intelligent Frederick Douglass was.

The words of Frederick Douglass
Frederick Douglass was a former slave who became a great spokesperson for the abolitionist cause.

Human government is for the protection of rights; and when human government destroys human rights, it ceases to be a government . . . If you look over the list of your rights, you do not find among them any right to make a slave of your brother.

Numbers should not be looked to so much as right. The man who is right is a majority. He who has God and conscience on his side, has a majority against the universe. . . . If he does not represent what we are, he represents what we ought to be . . .

The Liberator
In the first issue of *The Liberator,* William Lloyd Garrison stated that he would be very direct and honest about slavery.

I *will* be harsh as truth, and as uncompromising as justice. On this subject, I do not wish to think, to speak, or write, with moderation. . . . I am in earnest—I will not equivocate [deceive]— I will not excuse—I will not retreat a single inch—AND I WILL BE HEARD.

William Lloyd Garrison's abolitionist newspaper, *The Liberator*, was widely read and very influential in the North.

THE LIBERATOR.

VOL. I.] WILLIAM LLOYD GARRISON AND ISAAC KNAPP, PUBLISHERS. [NO. 17.

BOSTON, MASSACHUSETTS.] OUR COUNTRY IS THE WORLD—OUR COUNTRYMEN ARE MANKIND. [SATURDAY, APRIL 23, 1831.

35

Resistance and Rebellion

The most common form of resistance was for slaves to simply not work as hard as they were capable of working. President George Washington wrote that as soon as his **overseers** would turn their backs, slaves would stop working. According to many accounts left by former slaves, this was done on purpose. Small acts of **sabotage** and minor thefts were also frequently used to fight back against masters.

Despite rigid controls over slaves, there were some large **rebellions.** Louisiana, South Carolina, Florida, and other Southern states had major slave rebellions. Nat Turner's Rebellion is the best known in the United States. It took place in 1831 in Virginia. The only large, successful slave rebellion in modern times to permanently overthrow a government was the slave rebellion in Haiti. After each of these incidents, laws in slave-holding states became increasingly strict.

By the late 1700s, there were huge **plantations** in what is known today as Haiti. A very small group of Frenchmen controlled vast numbers of slaves on these lands. Several slaves were able to escape and hide in rugged mountains surrounding the farms. The brilliant leadership of escaped slave Touissant L'Ouvrture led to rebellion. Bloody battles were fought, but the slaves in Haiti eventually won and formed their own government in 1804.

Similar to the Haitian rebellion, in 1831 escaped slaves in Virginia also acquired weapons and then organized for a **revolt.** Nat Turner led the escaped slaves in raids on several plantations, but the Virginia **militia** stopped him and his followers. Approximately 59 whites and 100 blacks lost their lives in the fighting. Turner and his followers were convicted in trials and executed. Again, laws and controls on slaves were strengthened in the South.

In 1839, a slave **mutiny** occurred aboard the slave ship *Amistad. Amistad* was transporting slaves in the **West Indies.** Suddenly, the slaves rose up and took control of the ship. They tried to return to Africa, but the European crew tricked them and the ship ended up in the United States. The slaves sued for their freedom. Former President John Quincy Adams argued their case, and won.

A rebel speaks

Below, an unidentified slave—who was captured after taking part in Gabriel's Rebellion in Virginia, in August 1800—explains his actions.

I have nothing more to offer than what General [George] Washington would have had to offer, had he been taken by the British officers and put to trial by them. I have ventured my life in endeavouring [trying] to obtain the liberty of my countrymen, and am a willing sacrifice to their cause.

Post-rebellion thoughts

After Turner's Rebellion James McDonnell, a slave owner, spoke to the Virginia **legislature**.

[The Turner Rebellion raised the] suspicion that a Nat Turner might be in every family, that the same bloody deeds might be acted over at any time in any place, that the material for it was spread through-out the land, and always ready for a like explosion.

Death of Capt. Ferrer, the Captain of the Amistad, July, 1839.

Don Jose Ruiz and Don Pedro Montez, of the Island of Cuba, having purchased fifty-three slaves at Havana, recently imported from Africa, put them on board the Amistad, Capt. Ferrer, in order to transport them to Principe, another port on the Island of Cuba. After being out from Havana about four days, the African captives on board, in order to obtain their freedom, and return to Africa, armed themselves with cane knives, and rose upon the Captain and crew of the vessel. Capt. Ferrer and the cook of the vessel were killed; two of the crew escaped; Ruiz and Montez were made prisoners.

Thirty-five slaves were able to return to their African homelands as a result of the mutiny on the *Amistad*.

John Brown and Dred Scott

Among the most famous and controversial figures connected with slavery in the United States were John Brown and Dred Scott. These two men did much to bring attention to the plight of slaves. Both also had famous court trials. John Brown sought freedom for all slaves; Dred Scott sought freedom for himself.

In 1856, John Brown and his followers brutally murdered pro-slavery men in Kansas. In 1859, he tried to capture weapons and ammunition so he could lead a slave **revolt** throughout the South. He was captured at Harper's Ferry, Virginia (now West Virginia), convicted of **treason,** and executed. This incident was one of the main events that led to the Civil War.

Dred Scott was a slave. He got the idea to claim his freedom when his master took him to live in Illinois, and then Fort Snelling in the Wisconsin Territory—both places where slavery was illegal. Scott claimed that since he lived where slavery was illegal (and thus he could not have been a slave), he should be given freedom. The case went all the way to the U.S. Supreme Court, but Scott lost. In 1857, the court said that Scott's master could not be deprived of his property—meaning Scott— even though slavery was illegal in Illinois.

Abolitionists were outraged that Scott lost his case, while supporters of slavery were surprised that the courts had even considered Scott's case.

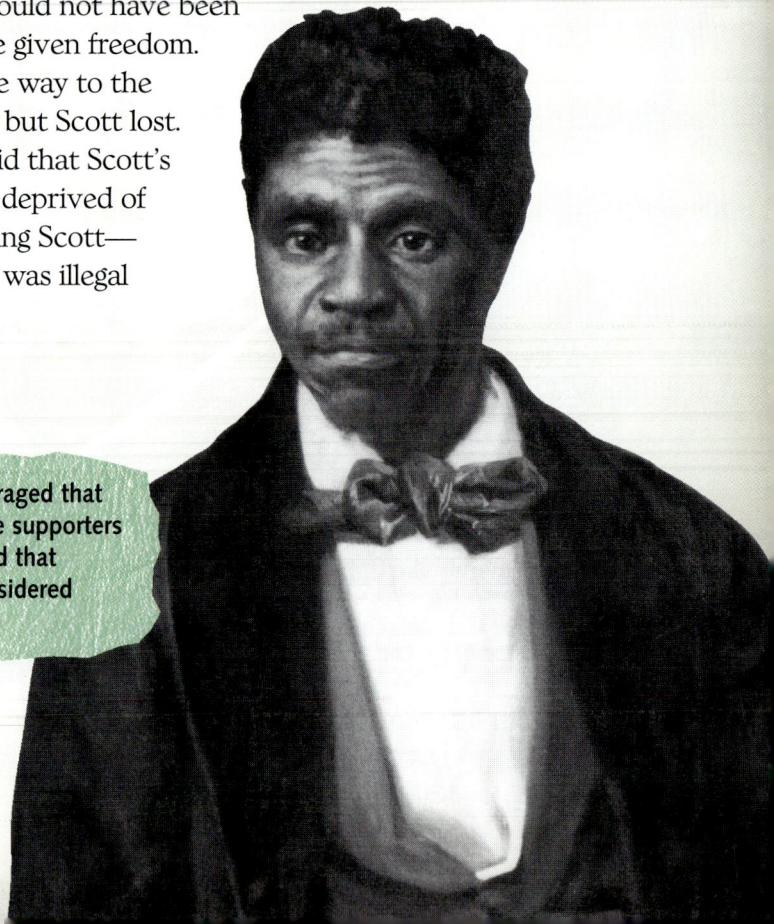

John Brown's trial
John Brown's trial was covered extensively by newspapers from all over the United States. The following is from his testimony.

I wish to say that you had better—all you people of the South—prepare yourselves for a settlement of this question. You may dispose of me very easily—I am nearly disposed of now; but this question is still to be settled— this negro question I mean; the end of that is not yet.

To some Americans, John Brown is considered one of the greatest heroes to fight against slavery in the United States. To others, he is considered a deranged murderer.

John Brown's last words
This is a note Brown handed to his executioner shortly before he was hanged on December 2, 1859.

Now it is deemed necessary that I should forfeit my life, for the furtherence of the ends of justice, and mingle my blood further with the blood of my children, and with the blood of millions in this slave country, whose rights are disregarded by wicked, cruel, and unjust enactments—I say let it be done!

From the governor
Henry Wise was governor of Virginia during the raid on Harper's Ferry. He was present at Brown's trial.

They are themselves mistaken who take him to be a madman. . . . He is a man of clear head, of courage, of fortitude and simple in genius.

Liberia

Many people in both the North and the South could tell that slavery was wrong and bad for the United States. Some people were **prejudiced** against Africans, and doubted they were capable of living and working in American society. Others felt that even if slaves could function properly, there would be conflict between whites and blacks.

Thomas Jefferson, James Monroe, and many others believed that slaves should be **liberated** and returned to Africa. In 1816, the American Colonization Society was formed. The goal of the American Colonization Society was to send freed slaves back to their native homes in Africa. The Society bought land on the west coast of Africa, and former slaves were settled there. That land became the country of Liberia. Its capital was named Monrovia in honor of one of its major supporters: James Monroe.

About 10,000 African Americans moved to Liberia. However, this was a very small percentage of the slaves living in the United States at the time. James Monroe, Henry Clay, and other prominent Americans supported the project. The expense of transportation and the unwillingness of many free blacks to go to Liberia eventually doomed this "back to Africa" movement. By 1865, there were almost no African Americans settling in Liberia, in part because they were used to life in the United States. Obviously slaves wanted freedom, but they wanted to stay in the United States. Liberia still exists today, but it is a poor nation with an unstable government.

The journey from the U.S. to Liberia is more than 4,000 miles (7,000 kilometers). Many slaves did not want to travel back to Africa.

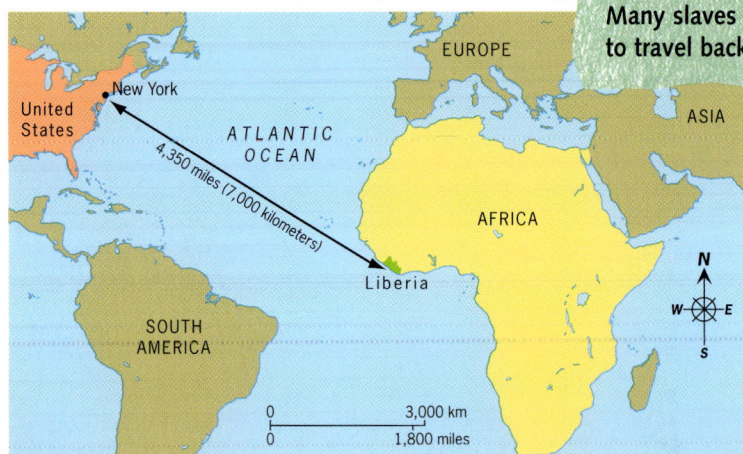

Avoiding a slavery solution?
William Lloyd Garrison commented on the American Colonization Society. He pointed out that the U.S. could avoid freeing slaves and providing them with equal treatment by sending them back to Africa.

[The American Colonization Society had] inflicted a great injury upon the free and slave population; first by strengthening the prejudices of the people; secondly, by discouraging the education of those who are free; thirdly, by inducing passage of severe **legislative** enactments; and, finally by lulling the whole country into a deep sleep.

Another opinion
William Wells Brown wrote the following in Massachusetts in the 1860s. It calls for freed slaves to emigrate—move to another land—and disputes arguments that they should stay in the United States.

All the objections to emigrations appear to centre in the feeling that we ought not to quit the land of our birth . . . If it could be shown that our presence here was actually needed, and that we could exert an influence . . . then I agree that duty would require us to remain. . . . [However,] the colored people of this country, are a **race** of cooks, waiters, barbers, whitewashers, bootblacks, and chimney sweeps. How much influence has such a class upon the community? . . . I hold that the descendants of Africa, in this country, will never be respected until they shall leave the cook shop and barber's chair and the whitewash brush . . . To emigrate to Haytii [Haiti], and to develop the resources of the Island, and to build up a powerful and influential government there, which shall demonstrate the genius and capabilities of the Negro, is as good an Anti-Slavery work as can be done in the Northern States of this Union.

The Underground Railroad

The Underground Railroad was a series of homes, barns, and other hiding places that provided safe areas where slaves could rest and be fed as they made their way north. Canada, which outlawed slavery in 1833, was often their destination. Most escaping slaves traveled at night and slept during the day to avoid detection. Volunteers hid runaways in barns, cellars, and other secret sites. They fed slaves and gave them directions to the next safe place. When Southern slave owners discovered that the Underground Railroad existed, they were furious.

Leaders of the Underground Railroad became known as conductors. Isaac T. Hopper from Philadelphia was one of the first conductors to help slaves escape. He began helping slaves escape while still a teenager in the 1780s. Another slave, John Mason, helped approximately 1,300 slaves to their freedom. The most famous leader of the Underground Railroad was Harriet Tubman. To prevent capture, she would start her journeys with escaped slaves on Saturday night—knowing that it was hard to raise search parties on Sunday.

Federal **fugitive** slave laws required that runaway slaves be returned to their masters if law officials discovered them. Often these returned slaves would face harsh punishment by their masters. But countless escaped slaves made it to safety thanks to Harriet Tubman and other brave volunteers.

Some slaves were hidden in specially built wagons with secret compartments. One slave, named Henry Brown, was hidden in a box and mailed to freedom.

Harriet Tubman remembers

Harriet Tubman, once a slave herself, helped hundreds of slaves escape on the Underground Railroad.

I had reasoned this out in my mind, there was one of two things I had a right to, liberty or death; if I could not have one, I would have the other. . . . I had crossed the line. I was free; but there was no one to welcome me to the land of freedom. I was a stranger in a strange land. . . . When I found I had crossed the [Mason-Dixon] line, I looked at my hands to see if I were the same person . . . the sun came like gold through the tree and over the field and I felt like I was in heaven.

Harriet Tubman, a free slave who had escaped from Maryland, did much to organize the Underground Railroad and help thousands of other slaves escape.

Abolitionist Writers

In 1857, an **abolitionist** named Harriet Beecher Stowe wrote *Uncle Tom's Cabin,* based on a serial she wrote for a magazine. She had never traveled to a Southern **plantation,** but wanted to dramatize how brutal slavery could be. Her book was widely read and created a sudden wave of abolitionist support among Northerners. Many famous writers such as Walt Whitman and Louisa May Alcott also spoke out against slavery. William Lloyd Garrison and Frederick Douglass emerged as the debate over slavery intensified. These writers strongly influenced U.S. society in the mid-1800s.

William Lloyd Garrison was an outstanding leader of the abolitionist movement, but at the time he only had a small following. People thought he was too radical—not only calling for slaves' freedom, but also requesting immediate equality to whites. Gradually, American beliefs in the North became more supportive of Garrison and his cause. This was in great part because of strong objections from Southerners. As more pro slavery people **protested** abolitionist writings and actions, even more people in the North began to see the evils of slavery.

Harriet Beecher Stowe was harshly criticized by Southerners for *Uncle Tom's Cabin* being inaccurate. However, as she prepared her novel, she interviewed former slaves so she could be realistic with descriptions.

Uncle Tom's Cabin: Mr. and Mrs. Shelby
Arthur and Emily Shelby were slave owners in Kentucky. Here, Mrs. Shelby discusses her thoughts on slavery with her husband.

"This is God's curse on slavery!—a bitter, bitter, most accursed thing!—a curse to the master and a curse to the slave! I was a fool to think I could make anything good out of such a deadly evil. It is a sin to hold a slave under laws like ours,—I always felt it was,—I always thought so when I was a girl,—I thought so still more after I joined the church; but I thought I could gild it over,—I thought, by kindness, and care, and instruction, I could make the condition of mine better than freedom—fool that I was!"

"Why, wife, you are getting to be an abolitionist, quite."

"Abolitionist! if they knew all I know about slavery, they might talk! We don't need them to tell us; you know I never thought that slavery was right—never felt willing to own slaves."

Uncle Tom's Cabin: Topsy and Miss Ophelia
Topsy—an eight-year-old slave—was given to Miss Ophelia by her cousin, St. Clare. Below, Topsy has stolen a ribbon and Miss Ophelia asks her why.

"Poor Topsy, why need you steal? You're going to be taken good care of now. I'm sure I'd rather give you anything of mine, than have you steal it."

It was the first word of kindness the child had ever heard in her life; and the sweet tone and manner struck strangely on the wild, rude heart, and a sparkle of something like a tear shone in the keen, round, glittering eye; but it was followed by the short laugh and habitual grin. No! the ear that has never heard anything but abuse is strangely incredulous [unwilling to accept what is offered as true] of anything so heavenly as kindness; and Topsy only thought Eva's speech something funny and inexplicable,—she did not believe it.

African-American Soldiers in the Civil War

African Americans fought in both the Northern and the Southern armies during the Civil War. Free blacks in the North wanted to fight as soon as the war began, but were stopped partially because of **prejudice** among military officials. So they worked at various tasks away from enemy lines in the first part of the war. Meanwhile, many trained hard, hoping to get a chance to fight. In the last two years of the war, free slaves were allowed in combat and they served with great distinction. In the last year of the war, several attempts were made to permit slaves to fight for the Confederacy. This met with little success.

As the Civil War dragged on, it became harder to attract enough soldiers to fight. Riots broke out in New York City and other places in the North in opposition to the **draft.** Finally, in 1862, African Americans were allowed to take part in combat. By the end of the war, more than 188,000 African Americans had fought for the North.

This group of African-Americans was photographed aboard the USS *Vermont* during the Civil War.

Lieutenant John Appleton's memories

Lieutenant John Appleton recorded the attack on Fort Wagner, South Carolina, in his diary. Appleton was one of the white officers serving with the African-American 54th Massachusetts troops. He described their performance in one of the bloodiest battles of the war.

"Prove yourselves, men," said the colonel as we started. Our lines were about sixteen hundred yards [1,463 meters] from the fort. As we advanced fire was opened upon us. . . . The fire became terrible—shell, canister, and musket balls tore through us. . . . The terrible was deafened us, as we pressed on, at last, we reached the moat of the fort. The men ran up the steep, earthen slope and stone wall of the fort under fire. On the top of the works we met the Rebels [Confederate troops] and by the flashes of the guns we looked down into the fort, apparently a sea of bayonets. The colonel planted the colors [flag].

General James Blunt's memories

General James Blunt commanded troops of the 1st Kansas Colored Regiment. He wrote the following after the July 17, 1863, battle at Honey Springs, Indian Territory, in what is now Oklahoma.

I never saw much fighting as was done by the Negro regiment. . . . The question that negroes will fight is settled; besides they make better soldiers in every respect than any troops I have ever had under my command. You have no idea how my prejudices with regard to Negro troops have been dispelled by the battle the other day.

Freed Slaves

Abraham Lincoln's main goal during his presidency was to keep the United States unified. He wanted to find a peaceful solution to slavery. Even after the Civil War started, Lincoln tried to keep his position on slavery neutral so the South would remain in the Union. By January 1863, he changed his tactics and issued the Emancipation Proclamation. The document declared that all slaves in the Confederacy were free. The **abolition** of slavery now became a prime **objective** of the war. It was the first major step toward making laws that freed all slaves in the United States.

The Thirteenth Amendment

When the Civil War ended in 1865, Congress and President Andrew Johnson—who became president when Lincoln was assassinated in April 1865—pushed to pass a Constitutional **amendment** that freed all slaves. This was the Thirteenth Amendment. It simply stated that slavery was no longer legal in the United States.

The Thirteenth Amendment freed slaves, but two more amendments were soon passed—the 14th and 15th —to make former slaves citizens and ensure voting rights.

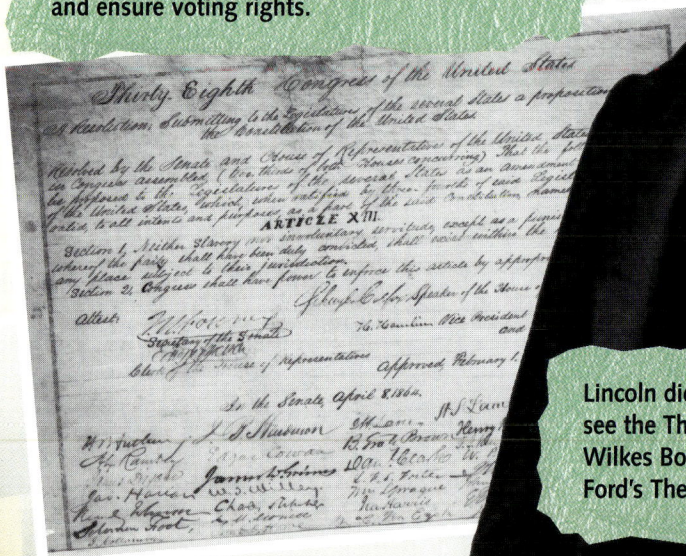

Lincoln did not live long enough to see the Thirteenth Amendment. John Wilkes Booth assassinated him in Ford's Theater on April 14, 1865.

The Emancipation Proclamation
Lincoln issued the Emancipation Proclamation in response to Confederate states not returning to the Union.

And by virtue of the power and for the purpose aforesaid, I do order and declare that all persons held as slaves within said designated States and parts of States are, and henceforward shall be, free; and that the Executive Government of the United States, including the military and naval authorities thereof, shall recognize and maintain the freedom of said persons.

And I hereby enjoin upon the people so declared to be free to abstain from all violence, unless in necessary self-defense; and I recommend to them that, in all cases where allowed, they labor faithfully for reasonable wages.

And I further declare and make known that such persons of suitable condition will be received into the armed service of the United States to garrison forts, positions, stations, and other places, and to man vessels of all sorts in said service. . . .

The Thirteenth Amendment
The Thirteenth Amendment to the Constitution officially ended slavery in the United States.

Section 1. Neither slavery nor involuntary **servitude**, except as a punishment for crime whereof the party shall have been duly convicted, shall exist within the United States, or any place subject to their jurisdiction.

Section 2. Congress shall have power to enforce this article by appropriate legislation.

What Have We Learned from Slavery?

There is still much to be learned about the practice of slavery. In the past, detailed records were not kept and the subject was often avoided. But we do know that the time period during which slavery existed was one of the most shameful chapters in United States history. It is tragic that U.S. leaders could not find a way to end slavery short of engaging in a bloody civil war.

Questions about slavery remain

In our study of history we can usually find out what happened. But finding out why things happened is often difficult. Why did people feel it was right to own slaves? Why couldn't a compromise be found to gradually end slavery? And, after the slaves were freed, why were African Americans denied basic rights for another 100 years? These questions are hard to answer.

Although the 13th, 14th, and 15th Amendments guaranteed former slaves equal rights, years of **protests** were needed to attain equal treatment in the United States.

Martin Luther King Jr.'s dream

About 100 years after slavery ended in the United States—August 28, 1963—the famous **civil rights** leader Martin Luther King Jr. delivered his most famous speech from the steps of the Lincoln Memorial in Washington, D.C. In this excerpt, he talks about his hopes for the future.

Five score [100] years ago, a great American [Abraham Lincoln], in whose symbolic shadow we stand today, signed the Emancipation Proclamation. This momentous [important] decree came as a great beacon light of hope to millions of Negro slaves, . . .

But one hundred years later, the Negro still is not free. One hundred years later, the life of the Negro is still sadly crippled by the manacles [hand cuffs] of **segregation** and the chains of **discrimination.** One hundred years later, the Negro lives on a lonely island of poverty in the midst of a vast ocean of material prosperity [**economic** success]. One hundred years later, the Negro is still languished [suffering neglect] in the corners of American society and finds himself an exile [outcast] in his own land.

I have a dream that one day this nation will rise up and live out the true meaning of its creed; we hold these truths to be self-evident that all men are created equal.

I have a dream, that one day . . . the sons of former slaves and the sons of former slave owners will be able to sit down together at the table of brotherhood.

I have a dream, that my four little children will one day live in a nation where they will not be judged by the color of their skin but by the content of their character.

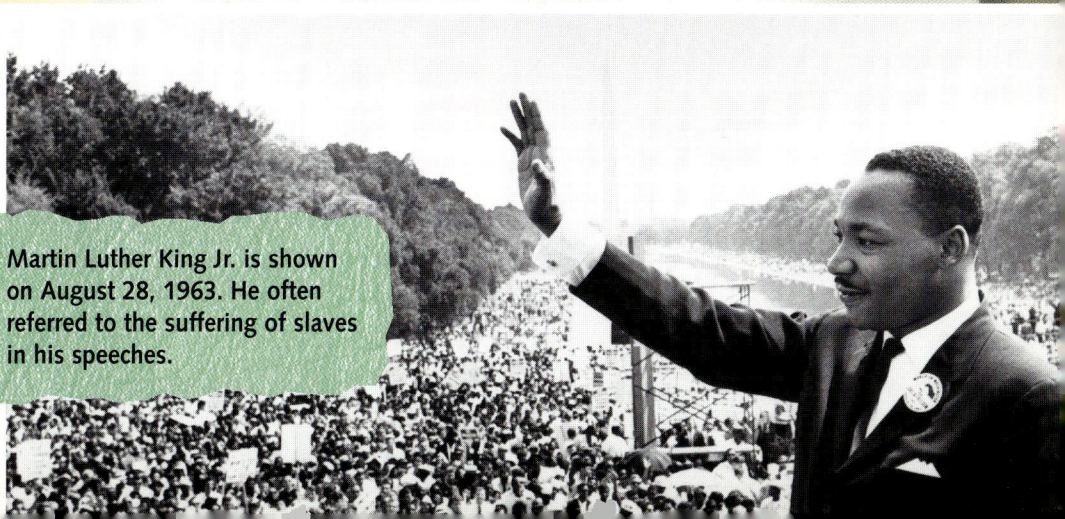

Martin Luther King Jr. is shown on August 28, 1963. He often referred to the suffering of slaves in his speeches.

Timeline

1619	The first Africans arrive in Jamestown, Virginia, as **indentured servants.**
1641	Massachusetts Bay and Plymouth are the first colonies to authorize slavery through laws.
1662	The Colony of Virginia passes a law that says children of African-American women are slaves if their mothers were slaves.
1688	**Quakers protest** slavery in Germantown, Pennsylvania.
1776	The Declaration of Independence states that all men are created equal, but says nothing about the practice of slavery.
1777-1804	Slavery is gradually **abolished** in Vermont, Massachusetts, New Hampshire, Pennsylvania, Rhode Island, Connecticut, New York, and New Jersey.
1787	The **Northwest Ordinance** allows slavery in western states south of the Ohio River.
1789	The U.S. Constitution is adopted and allows slavery to continue.
1793	The first federal **fugitive** slave law requires that escaped slaves be returned across state borders if caught.
1794	The **cotton gin** is invented by Eli Whitney and increases demand for slaves.
1804	Haitian slaves conduct a victorious **revolt** against the French.
1808	A law passed by Congress takes effect stating it is illegal to bring any more slaves from Africa to the United States.
1816	The American Colonization Society is organized; it encourages free blacks in the United States to return to and settle in Liberia.
1821	A slave revolt in Charleston, South Carolina, is led by free African American Denmark Vesey.
1831	William Lloyd Garrison begins publishing an **abolitionist** paper, *The Liberator*. The Nat Turner **Rebellion** takes place in Virginia.
1832	Slavery ends in the British Empire.
1837	Abolitionist Elijah P. Lovejoy is murdered by a mob in Alton, Illinois, for opposing slavery.
1839	A slave **mutiny** occurs on the slave ship *Amistad.*
1841	Frederick Douglass's first antislavery speech makes him a leading abolitionist.
1849	Harriet Tubman escapes from slavery; she later becomes a conductor on the Underground Railroad.
1850	The Compromise of 1850 is passed by Congress.
1851	*Uncle Tom's Cabin*, a popular antislavery novel, is written by Harriet Beecher Stowe.
1856	The **Republican Party** forms as an antislavery political party.
1857	In the Dred Scott case, the U.S. Supreme Court rules that Congress cannot deprive citizens of their slaves.
1858	John Brown and his followers raid the arsenal at Harper's Ferry, Virginia, and try to start a slave revolt. He is captured and executed.
1861	The Civil War begins after Southern states **secede** from the Union and attack Fort Sumter, South Carolina.
1862	President Abraham Lincoln's Emancipation Proclamation takes effect, freeing slaves in the Confederacy.
1863	African-American soldiers are allowed in the Union army. The Massachusetts 54th Regiment leads a heroic attack on Fort Wagner, South Carolina.
1865	The Civil War ends with a Northern victory. Abraham Lincoln is assassinated by John Wilkes Booth. Congress passes the Thirteenth Amendment, which abolishes slavery in the United States.

List of Primary Sources

The author and publisher gratefully acknowledge the following publications and websites from which written sources in this book are drawn. In some cases, the wording or sentence structure has been simplified to make the material more appropriate for a school readership.

p. 9 William Buckland: www.iath.virginia.edu/vcdh/jamestown/wbind1.html.
   Richard Allen: *Autobiography of a People*, Herb Boyd (New York: Doubleday, 2000).
p. 11 John Rolfe: www.history.org.
   Virginia General Assembly: statement (1705) from *Africans in America: America's Journey through Slavery*, Charles Johnson, Patricia Smith, and the WGBH Series Research Team (New York: Harcourt, Brace, and Company, 1998).
p. 13 James Albert Ukawsaw Gronniosaw: *Autobiography of a People*, Herb Boyd (New York: Doubleday, 2000).
   Reverend John Newton: *Historical Viewpoints, Volume One: To 1877, Notable Articles from American Heritage: The Magazine of History*, John A. Garraty (editor) (New York: American Heritage Publishing Co., Inc., 1970).
p. 15 William Wells Brown: *From Slavery to Freedom: A History of Negro Americans*, Sixth Edition, John Hope Franklin, and Alfred A. Moss Jr (New York: Alfred Knopf, 1988).
p. 17 Edmund Bacon: www.pbs.org.
   Mingo White: *Slavery Time: When I was Chillun*, Belinda Hurmence (New York: G. P. Putnam's Sons, 1997).
p. 19 Olaudah Equiano: *Autobiography of a People*, Herb Boyd (New York: Doubleday, 2000).
   Austin Stewart: *Autobiography of a People*, Herb Boyd (New York: Doubleday, 2000).
p. 21 Harriet Newby: *Slavery Time: When I was Chillun*, Belinda Hurmence (New York: G. P. Putnam's Sons, 1997).
   Mary Island: *Slavery Time: When I was Chillun*, Belinda Hurmence (New York: G. P. Putnam's Sons, 1997).
p. 23 Mary Reynolds: *The Civitas Anthology of African American Slave Narratives*, William L. Andrews and Henry Louis Gates Jr. (editors) (Washington, D.C.: Civitas Counterpoint, 1999).
   James Bolton: *Slavery Time: When I was Chillun*, Belinda Hurmence (New York: G. P. Putnam's Sons, 1997).
p. 25 Harriet Jacobs: *The Civitas Anthology of African American Slave Narratives*, William L. Andrews and Henry Louis Gates Jr. (editors) (Washington, D.C.: Civitas Counterpoint, 1999).
   Hannah Chapman: *Remembering Slavery: African Americans Talk about their Personal Experiences of Slavery and Freedom*, Ira Belin, Marc Favreau, and Steven F. Miller (editors) (New York: The New Press, 1998).
p. 27 William Craft: *William Craft: Running a Thousand Miles for Freedom* (London: William Tweedie, 1860).
   Gus Smith: *Slavery Time: When I was Chillun*, Belinda Hurmence (New York: G. P. Putnam's Sons, 1997).
p. 29 "Swing Low, Sweet Chariot."
p. 31 Abraham Lincoln: speech at Peoria, Illinois (October 16, 1854).
   Abraham Lincoln: speech at Republican State Convention, Springfield, Illinois (June 16, 1858).
   Abraham Lincoln: fragment (August 1, 1858?) from *The Collected Works of Abraham Lincoln* (vol. II), Roy P. Basler (New Brunswick, NJ: Rutgers University Press, 1990).
   Abraham Lincoln: letter to H. L. Pierce and others (April 6, 1859).
p. 33 Alabama Slave Code of 1852: The Code of Alabama, prepared by John J. Ormand, Arthur P. Bagby, and George Goldwaite (Montgomery, Ala.: Brittain and DeWolf, 1852).
   James Madison: letter to Harriet Martineau.
p. 35 Frederick Douglass: "Frederick Douglass's Paper" (August 1852) from *Voices of the Civil War: A Documentary History of the Great American Conflict*, Milton Meltzer (editor) (New York: Thomas Crowell, 1989).
   William Lloyd Garrison: from first issue of *The Liberator* (Boston, 1831).
p. 37 Unidentified slave involved in Gabriel's Rebellion: *From Slavery to Freedom: A History of Negro Americans*, Sixth Edition, John Hope Franklin and Alfred A. Moss Jr (New York: Alfred Knopf, 1988).
   James McDonnell: *Breaking the Chains: African-American Slave Resistance*, William Loren Katz (New York: Atheneum, 1990).
p. 39 John Brown:www.pbs.org/wgbh/amex/brown/filmmore/transcript/transcript1.html.
   John Brown: www.pbs.org/wgbh/amex/brown/filmmore/transcript/transcript1.html.
   Henry Wise: *From Slavery to Freedom: A History of Negro Americans*, Sixth Edition, John Hope Franklin, and Alfred A. Moss Jr (New York: Alfred Knopf, 1988).
p. 41 William Lloyd Garrison: *From Slavery to Freedom: A History of Negro Americans*, Sixth Edition, John Hope Franklin, and Alfred A. Moss Jr (New York: Alfred Knopf, 1988).
   William Wells Brown: *Autobiography of a People*, Herb Boyd (New York: Doubleday, 2000).
p. 43 Harriet Tubman: *Autobiography of a People*, Herb Boyd (New York: Doubleday, 2000).
p. 45 Harriet Beecher Stowe: *Uncle Tom's Cabin*, Harriet Beecher Stowe (New York: Bantam, 1982).
   Harriet Beecher Stowe: *Uncle Tom's Cabin*, Harriet Beecher Stowe (New York: Bantam, 1982).
p. 47 Lieutenant John Appleton: www.nd.nps.gov.
   General James Blunt: www.yale.edu.
p. 49 Abraham Lincoln: The Emancipation Proclamation (January 1, 1863).
   The Thirteenth Amendment of the United States Constitution (ratified December 18, 1865).
p. 51 Martin Luther King Jr.: speech at Lincoln Memorial, Washington, D.C. (August 28, 1963).

Glossary

abolish put an end to something

abolitionist person who actively worked to end slavery

agent representative

agriculture practice of cultivating of soil, producing of crops, and raising of livestock

amendment formal change, usually to a government document

auction public sale, usually involving bids by buyers

auctioneer person in charge of auctions

bias existing opinion about someone or something that makes it hard to be fair

bondage forced to obey another

civil rights nonpolitical rights of a citizen, especially the rights of personal liberty guaranteed by the 13th and 14th amendments to the Constitution

compromise cooperation whereby each side gives up something and gains something

cotton gin machine invented by Eli Whitney in 1793 that separates cotton seeds from cotton fibers

covenant formal or solemn agreement

debt something owed to another

discrimination favoring one group over another

draft to call up for required military service

entrenched well-established

economy way an economic system, such as a country or a period in history, is organized

flog beat or whip

fugitive escaping slave

indentured servant person who is temporarily a slave; after a certain number of years in service for his or her master, he or she receives freedom

industrial describes the production of goods by machines in factories

inferior of lower quality or ability

innovative inventive

legislature body of persons having the power to make, change, or cancel laws

liberate set free

manipulation skillfully use or misuse

Mason-Dixon Line boundary between Maryland and Pennsylvania, dividing Northern and Southern states

minority group group of people who have less power or fewer members than others

militia local or state military group

mulatto person of mixed white and black ancestry

mutiny uprising against established authority, usually on a ship

Northwest Ordinance 1787 act of Congress that established a method for states to join the Union

objective free of strong opinions and bias

overseer person hired by a plantation owner to supervise the running of the plantation

paternalism system in which authorities treat those under their control similarly to how a parent treats a child

plantation large farm or farm community

planter wealthy owner of farmland

port place where ships load or unload cargo

prejudice belief that one group is superior to another

prisoner of war person captured in war, usually a member of the armed forces of a nation who is taken by the enemy during combat

profit valuable gain, usually in money

protest complaint or objection against an idea, act, or a way of doing things

province part of a country having a government of its own

Quaker member of a group of Christians whose religious beliefs include an opposition to war

race group of individuals with the same ancestors

racism negative beliefs held or actions taken against a group of people specifically because they have different physical characteristics from others

ration limited portion of food allowed to a person

rebellion organized revolt against authority

revolt rebel against the authority of a ruler or government

Republican Party group that believes that supreme power lies in the citizens through their right to vote

Roman Empire lands and people under the rule of ancient Rome

sabotage cause damage through a secret attack

secession breaking away from a country or organization

self-sufficient able to live without help from others

servitude condition of a slave

slave block site where slaves were sold

slave trader person who sold slaves

tradition long-time custom followed by a group of people

treason betray one's country or group to an enemy

West Indies chain of islands that divides the Caribbean Sea from the rest of the Atlantic Ocean. Some of the countries included in the West Indies are Cuba, Dominican Republic, Haiti, and Jamaica

Sources for Further Research

Isaacs, Sally Senzell. *America in the Time of Abraham Lincoln.* Chicago: Heinemann Library, 1999.

January, Brendan. *Civil Rights.* Chicago: Heinemann Library, 2004.

Riehecky, Janet. *The Emancipation Proclamation: The Abolition of Slavery.* Chicago: Heinemann Library, 2002.

Smolinski, Diane. *The Home Front in the North.* Chicago: Heinemann Library, 2001.

Smolinski, Diane. *The Home Front in the South.* Chicago: Heinemann Library, 2001.

Index